Frog and Friends

Best Summer Ever

Written by Eve Bunting

Illustrated by Josée Masse

For the LunchBunchers

—Eve

To my little star, Alice.

—Josée

This book has a reading comprehension level of 2.1 under the ATOS® readability formula.
For information about ATOS please visit www.renlearn.com.
ATOS is a registered trademark of Renaissance Learning, Inc.

Lexile®, Lexile® Framework and the Lexile® logo are trademarks of MetaMetrics, Inc.,
and are registered in the United States and abroad. The trademarks and names of other
companies and products mentioned herein are the property of their respective owners.
Copyright © 2010 MetaMetrics, Inc. All rights reserved.

Text Copyright © 2012 Eve Bunting
Illustration Copyright © 2012 Josée Masse

Sleeping Bear Press™

315 E. Eisenhower Parkway, Ste. 200
Ann Arbor, MI 48108
www.sleepingbearpress.com

Printed and bound in the United States.

10 9 8 7 6 5 4 3 2 (case)
10 9 8 7 6 5 4 3 2 (pbk)

Library of Congress Cataloging-in-Publication Data • Bunting, Eve, 1928- • Frog and friends : the best
summer ever / Eve Bunting; • Josée Masse. • p. cm. • Summary: Frog enjoys a summer with his friends
as he compares himself to a bat, takes a vacation, and meets a Starman who helps him to see the night
sky in a new way. • ISBN 978-1-58536-550-0 (hard cover) — ISBN 978-1-58536-691-0 (pbk.) • [1. Frogs-
-Fiction. 2. Animals--Fiction. 3. Friendship--Fiction. 4. Ponds--Fiction. 5. Summer--Fiction.] I. Masse,
Josée, ill. II. Title. III. Title: Best summer ever. • PZ7.B91527Fsb 2012 • [E]--dc23 • 2011030797

Table of Contents

Frog and Little Brown Bat

Sometimes at night Little Brown Bat

swooped down to visit Frog.

Sometimes they talked about how

different they were.

It was a game they liked to play.

"I swim and you do not," Frog said, not

unkindly.

"I fly and you do not," Little Brown Bat

said.

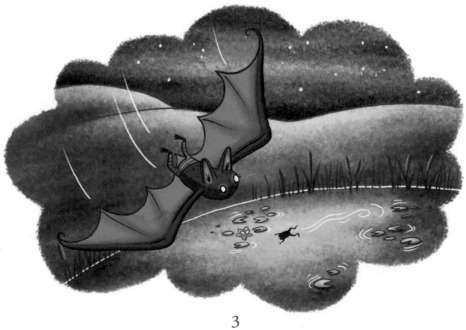

Frog nodded. "But I am a good leaper. Sometimes leaping feels like flying."

"I can understand that," Little Brown Bat said. "But I think it is prettier way up high in the night sky."

Frog sighed. "It may be. I cannot have everything."

They thought for awhile.

"We both love bugs. I catch them as I fly,"

Little Brown Bat said.

"I lie on my lily pad. I catch them on my long sticky tongue." Frog flicked out his tongue to show her.

"That is a very handsome tongue," Little Brown Bat said.

They stayed, talking in the soft, warm dark.

Little Brown Bat swung by her legs from the oak tree branch. Frog sat on the stone by his pond.

"Some people say I am ugly," Little Brown Bat said.

Frog shook his head. "You are not. You are dark and lovely. Some also say I am ugly. But once a girl wanted to kiss me."

"I am not surprised," Little Brown Bat said. "You have a very nice face."

Little Brown Bat wafted her wings. Frog felt the lift of wind. She was leaving.

"Now I must fly," Little Brown Bat said. "But I will be back soon."

"Goodbye," Frog said. "Au revoir."

Sometimes he liked to speak French.

"We must tell Rabbit goodbye," Raccoon said. "She will be sad that she cannot come. She cannot leave her new babies."

Frog sighed. "We do not want her to be sad. She can come. We can bring her babies. We can each carry one. Or two."

"yea! yea!" The little possums clapped their little paws.

They went to Rabbit's rabbit hole and called in.

"I think a vacation will be good for me," Rabbit said. "My babies will like it, too."

So Squirrel led the way. They carried

the babies. Jumping Mouse could not carry

any. The babies were bigger than she was.

They walked and hopped and ran and

swung through the trees.

"Here is the place," Squirrel said.

It was lovely. There was grass to eat,
and worms, and spiders and flies, and
berries, two kinds. There was something
for everyone.

The baby rabbits slept. Everyone wanted

to bunny-sit.

Rabbit slept, too, on the napping rock.

"I have been getting no sleep because of the

bunnies," she said.

When it began to get dark Frog said, "I think it is time to go home now."

"It was such a nice change," Chameleon said.

"Fun!" Possum agreed. "Fun is what vacations are for."

Frog nodded. "You are right."

Raccoon tied Frog's scarf in a bow. "Let us come again next year."

"Yes," Frog said. "It was the best vacation ever. Thank you all for coming with me."

"You are welcome," they said.

Frog felt all pepped up. A vacation was all he had needed.

Now he could go home and be alone and have thinking time.

Happy on his very own napping rock.

Starman looked around. "Is this your pond?"

"Yes."

"But you leave it where it is, right?"

"Yes," Frog said.

"Is this your rock that you are sitting on?"

"Yes."

"But it has been here for years and years and years. Even before you were a tadpole."

"That is true," Frog said.

Then little Jumping Mouse said, "We can sing you a song about stars, if you like."

"I would like," Starman said.

They sang:

"*Twinkle, twinkle, little star,*

How I wonder what you are.

Up above the world so high,

Like a diamond in the sky."

They each sang to their own star, as if it were the only one in the sky. And Starman was right.

Frog was happy.

And he thought his star was happy, too.